# Nature Babies

### By Gina Ingoglia
### Illustrated by Lisa Bonforte

### A GOLDEN BOOK · NEW YORK
Western Publishing Company, Inc., Racine, Wisconsin 53404

Some places in the world are sunny. Others are icy and cold.

In some places it rains almost every day. In others it is sandy and dry.

But *every* place has baby animals!

Baby lions live where it's grassy and hot. Their mothers and fathers take very good care of them. Little lions play a lot with their mother—even when she is trying to rest!

Little tiger cubs don't like the heat. They take naps in the shade. Most cats don't like water, but tigers often lie in it to keep cool.

Newborn koalas and kangaroos stay in their mothers' pouches. It's like living in a pocket.

A young kangaroo climbs out of its mother's pouch to look for food. But it climbs back in to sleep.

A young koala rides on its mother's back
when it gets too big for the pouch.

Zebras and giraffes live where there's lots of room to run. Their babies can run very fast. These animals often drink together at muddy water holes.

Baby chimpanzees live in the forest. Their big nest is built in a tree. The whole family lives in it. Chimpanzees cover themselves with leaves to keep warm.

Gibbons live in trees, too. They have *very* long arms! The babies are always carried by their mothers. A baby gibbon hangs on tightly as its mother swings on the branches.

Baby elephants are hairy and pinkish-brown. They each weigh about 200 pounds! Elephants like to take baths in the river and squirt water out of their trunks. Little elephants follow their mothers everywhere.

Hippopotamus babies are sometimes born in the water. They spend most of their time there. But when it is not too hot, they lie on the riverbanks.

Rhinoceros babies live in grassy places close
to water. They eat leaves and twigs and grass.
Baby rhinos love to roll in the mud!

Little camels live in the hot desert. Their wide feet keep them from sinking into the sand. Camels have long eyelashes to keep the sand out of their eyes. Camels can close their noses during sandstorms.

Polar bears are born in the winter. They live with their mother in a den made of ice and snow. These tiny bears are very weak and no bigger than rabbits. But they grow up fast. By the end of the summer, they are big and strong.

Father and mother penguins keep their
eggs warm. They both take care of the babies
after they hatch. Baby penguins become
fast swimmers.

Gray seal babies are born with white fur.
Later it becomes gray with dark spots. The
fur keeps them warm in icy water. Seals like
to dry off in the sun.

The baby blue whale lives in the ocean. It is the biggest baby animal in the world. This baby is 23 feet long when it's born!

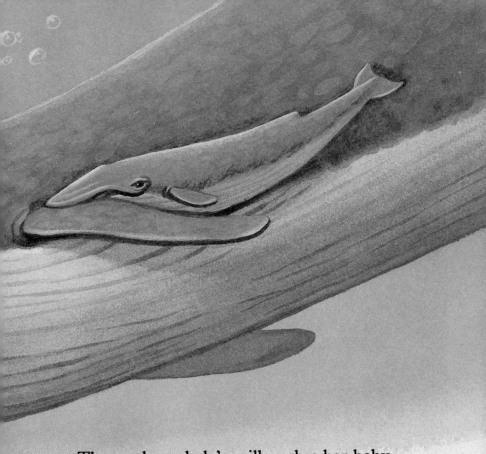

The mother whale's milk makes her baby grow even bigger. Baby whales can grow up to weigh as much as 24 elephants!

When baby animals grow up, they can take care of themselves. They can also take care of their *own* babies!